W9-APX-812

WILLIMANTIC PUBLIC LIBRARY

3 4036 05313 0583

398
HOU   House that Jack
                built

             The house that
             Jack built

DUE DATE

WILLIMANTIC PUBLIC LIBRARY
CHILDREN'S DEPARTMENT

THE HOUSE THAT JACK BUILT

A Mother Goose Nursery Rhyme

illustrated by

JANET STEVENS

Holiday House / New York

For Jack's house that he built and
for my new house and home.

J. S.

Illustrations copyright © 1985 by Janet Stevens
All rights reserved
Printed in the United States of America

Library of Congress Cataloging in Publication Data

House that Jack built.
   The house that Jack built.
   SUMMARY: A cumulative nursery rhyme about the chain
of events that started when Jack built a house.
   1. Nursery rhymes.   2. Children's poetry.   [1. Nursery
rhymes]   I. Stevens, Janet, ill.   II. Title.
PZ8.3.H79   1985   398'.8   84-15832
ISBN 0-8234-0548-6

WILLIMANTIC PUBLIC LIBRARY
CHILDREN'S DEPARTMENT
95-0407

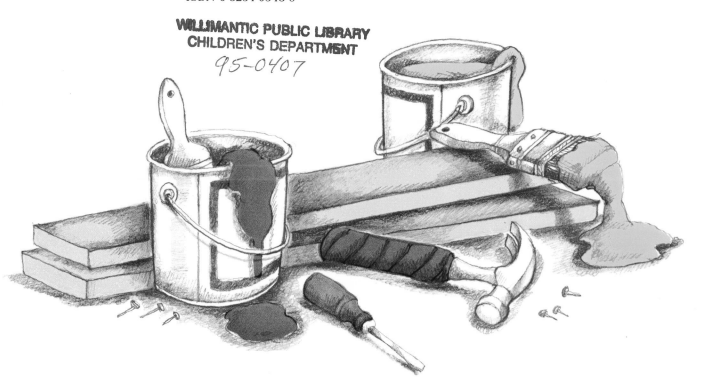

HOUSE

This is the house that Jack built.

MALT

This is the malt

That lay in the house
that Jack built.

RAT

This is the rat,

That ate the malt

That lay in the house
that Jack built.

CAT

This is the cat,

That killed the rat,

That ate the malt

That lay in the house
that Jack built.

DOG

This is the dog,

That worried the cat,

That killed the rat,

That ate the malt

That lay in the house
that Jack built.

COW

This is the cow with the crumpled horn,

That tossed the dog,

That worried the cat,

That killed the rat,

That ate the malt

That lay in the house
that Jack built.

MAIDEN

This is the maiden all forlorn,

That milked the cow
with the crumpled horn,

That tossed the dog,

That worried the cat,

That killed the rat,

That ate the malt

That lay in the house
that Jack built.

MAN

This is the man all tattered and torn,

That kissed the maiden
all forlorn,

That milked the cow
with the crumpled horn,

That tossed the dog,

That worried the cat,

That killed the rat,

That ate the malt

That lay in the house
that Jack built.

PRIEST

This is the priest all shaven and shorn,

That married the man
all tattered and torn,

That kissed the maiden
all forlorn,

That milked the cow
with the crumpled horn,

That tossed the dog,

That worried the cat,

That killed the rat,

That ate the malt

That lay in the house
that Jack built.

COCK

This is the cock that crowed in the morn,

That waked the priest
all shaven and shorn,

That married the man
all tattered and torn,

That kissed the maiden
all forlorn,

That milked the cow
with the crumpled horn,

That tossed the dog,

That worried the cat,

That killed the rat,

That ate the malt

That lay in the house
that Jack built.

FARMER

This is the farmer sowing the corn,

That kept the cock
that crowed in the morn,

That waked the priest
all shaven and shorn,

That married the man
all tattered and torn,

That kissed the maiden
all forlorn,

That milked the cow
with the crumpled horn,

That tossed the dog,

That worried the cat,

That killed the rat,

That ate the malt

That lay in the house that Jack built.